The Frog Prince

Illustrated by Mike and Carl Gordon

Retold by Susanna Davidson

Based on the fairytale by the Brothers Grimm

Designed by Samantha Meredith

Princess Poppy was furious. "I WON'T marry
Prince Humperdink," she said.

"He's smelly and smug
and slimier than a frog."

"You don't have to marry him now," said her mother.
"You just have to marry him when you grow up."

"I never want to marry him," said Poppy.
"I'd rather eat my toenails."

"I'll find another prince to marry," she snapped.

"You can have until tomorrow morning," said the King.
"But you'll never find a prince in that time."

"Just you wait," said Poppy.

And she stomped into the garden with her golden ball.

Poppy was so cross, she didn't see the wobbly stone.

She wibbled...

she wobbled...

She slipped and fell...

SPLAT!

...face-first into the pond.

Her golden ball plopped into the water.
"Help! I'm in big trouble now," wailed Poppy.

"Oh no you're not," croaked a frog.
"I can help you!"

FROGGY HERE WILL
SAVE YOUR BALL.

"But in return..." said the frog.

"...I want to live
in your palace,
eat from your plate
and sleep on your silken pillow."

"In your dreams," thought Poppy.

But out loud she said,
"I promise."

As soon as the frog gave
Poppy her ball, she raced
back to the palace.

Poppy arrived just in time for dinner.
She had to sit next to Prince Humperdink,
who smelled of cabbage.

Then, to Poppy's horror, she heard a
Splat... Splat... Splat...
In hopped the frog.

Go away!

"Excuse me," said the frog.
"Princess Poppy promised I could stay with her."

"And princesses don't break promises,"
bellowed the King. "The frog is our guest."

"Thank you," said the frog, diving into Poppy's soup.

I don't think I'm hungry anymore.

"Now," said the frog, when he'd
slurped up all the soup. "Time for bed."

"Oh no!" said Poppy. "You're not
coming anywhere near my bedroom."

"Princesses don't break promises," repeated the King.

So Princess Poppy picked up the frog and dropped him in the darkest, most distant corner of her room...

"But Princess Poppy,"
said the frog, "you promised
I could sleep on your bed."

IF YOU DON'T LET ME, I'LL TELL YOUR FATHER!

"I've had enough!" snapped Princess Poppy.
"You're the meanest, most horrible frog I've EVER met."

And with that, she threw
the frog out the window.

There was a long
silence, followed by
a loud **SPLAT**.

"Oh no!" thought Poppy.
"What have I done?"

She rushed outside
and picked up the frog,
as gently as she could.

"I'm so sorry," said Poppy.
And she bent down and kissed him.
There was a loud **CRASH**
and a deafening **BANG!**

In the place of the frog, stood a handsome prince.

"How can I ever thank you?" asked the Prince.
"Well," said Poppy, "you could marry me."

"Excuse me," said
Prince Humperdink,
"but Poppy is going
to marry ME."

"Oh no I'm not," said Poppy.
"Daddy, you did say I could find my own prince...
and kings don't break promises either."

"That is true," sighed the King.

"In that case," said the Prince,
"Princess Poppy, will you marry me?"

"I will," said Princess Poppy.

And when she grew up she did...

...and they lived happily ever after.

Edited by Jenny Tyler and Lesley Sims
Digital manipulation by John Russell